# Junkyard Dan

## Taking Names and Kicking Assets

Elise Leonard

**NOX PRESS**
books for that extra kick to give you more power
www.NoxPress.com

Leonard, Elise
Junkyard Dan series / Taking Names and Kicking Assets
ISBN: 978-1-935366-06-5

Copyright © 2010 by Elise Leonard.
All rights reserved, including the right of reproduction in whole or in part in any form. Published by Nox Press.
www.NoxPress.com

First Nox Press printing: September 2010

books for that extra kick to give you more power

This book is dedicated to the
**Harris County Juvenile Probation Department**
in Texas.

Particularly to Henry Gonzales,
Assistant Executive Director,
who is, in my humble opinion,
one of those rare administrators
who **truly** cares about the kids he serves,
putting their needs and education above all else.
It is an honor to know you, Henry.

And speaking of those who care about the kids they
serve, this book is also dedicated to Diane Hubbell,
Ellen Savoy and Oliver Burbridge, Jr.

Of course, the key to success flows down to the most
important person in each learner's life, the educator.

So this book has a special dedication to
Ms. Rosemary Holladay at Youth Village.
You are, without doubt, a born educator.
Your dedication to and your love for your students
is evident not only in your everyday teaching,
but it is clearly documented in your 96% success rate.
(Keep at it, and you **will** get to a 100% success rate.) ☺

But despite any great administrators and educators,
there would be no learning if not for the learners.
So this book is *really* for Ms. Holladay's students.
You guys liked the blue Lotus... so here you go.
I heard you guys worked hard and kicked school butt!
Congratulations, guys! I'm so very proud of you.

*~Elise*

## Chapter 1

"Have you seen Bubba?" Rosa asked.

I grinned.

"Too often."

"Know where he is now?" she asked.

I looked at my door.

Like clockwork, he appeared.

Bubba barreled through the door.

"Yo. Dude. What's hanging?!" he said.

Rosa looked at me and laughed.

"How did you do that?" she asked me.

I sighed loudly.

"You asked the wrong question," I told Rosa.

She laughed again, making a light tinkling sound.

"What was the right question?" she asked.

I thought about that, then I answered her.

"The right question is... 'When is Bubba *not* around?'"

Rosa laughed at that.

I did too.

But as usual, Bubba didn't get my point.

"Yeah. I'm like a genie," Bubba said. "I'm always around when you need me."

I looked at Bubba. My face was blank.

"You're just always around," I said.

"Because you need me," Bubba added.

"No. Most likely because it's mealtime," I muttered.

"Speaking of which," Bubba said. "I'm starved."

I looked at Rosa.

"I rest my case," was all I said.

Rosa cracked up.

She followed Bubba to my kitchen.

## Taking Names and Kicking Assets

I followed both of them.

"I heard someone put my name in for sheriff," Rosa said to Bubba's back.

He was looking through my cabinets.

"Really?" he said.

His voice had cracked.

Even *I* could tell he was up to something. (Besides stealing my food.)

"Yes," Rosa said calmly. "Really."

"Hm," Bubba said.

Rosa looked at me.

Then she grinned and winked.

She nodded her head toward Bubba. Then she winked again.

It was as if she were saying, "Watch this."

She started spitting questions at him like bullets.

Fast and hard. Aimed straight at him.

"So. You didn't know I was put up for sheriff?"

"No."

"And you don't know who entered my

name?"

"No."

"You have no clue?"

"No."

"Was there anything I could do about it?"

"No."

"Was there anything you could do about it?"

"No."

"So you were alone when you did it?"

"No."

"Who was with you?"

"Judge Simpkins."

Rosa stopped her questions.

Bubba tensed up.

Then he turned around slowly.

"Dang it!" he said loudly.

Rosa stared at Bubba.

"Are you mad?" he asked Rosa.

"Mad? As in insane? No. Do you want to know if I'm angry?"

Bubba looked at her with caution.

"Do I *want* to know?" he asked her softly.

## Taking Names and Kicking Assets

At first, she looked hard and mean. Just like a sheriff would look. You know, while they're trying to get info from a perp.

But then she smiled warmly.

"No," she said. "I'm not angry. In fact, I'm a little flattered."

That made me hopeful.

"So you'll take the job?" I asked her.

She looked at me head on.

"You don't just 'take' a sheriff's job. You have to be elected. People have to vote for you."

"You have nothing to eat in this place!" Bubba told me.

"So go somewhere else," I suggested. "Please."

"Nah," Bubba said.

I couldn't be so lucky.

If it were that easy to get rid of Bubba, I would have found a way by now.

## Chapter 2

Rosa turned to me.

"Would you like me to try to be sheriff?"

"I'd love it," I replied.

She was grinning.

So was I.

We were gazing at each other, each lost in thought.

I don't know what she was thinking, but I knew what I was thinking.

I was thinking thoughts of Rosa.

She was such a great woman.

She'd saved that boy Rico.

## Taking Names and Kicking Assets

He was now free.

And because of Rosa, many *other* people were free, too. All were released from prison.

People who deserved to be free, because they were innocent.

But Rosa was the only one who'd cared enough to solve those cases.

She was a good woman. A woman of honor.

Bubba let out a little yelp of joy.

He'd found my secret stash of chips.

In seconds, he was halfway through the entire bag.

I tried to ignore him, but it was hard.

But if I looked at Rosa, really focused on her, I could do it.

So that's what I did.

I gazed at Rosa.

My thoughts filled with warmth and pride.

"People, people," Bubba said. "Please. I'm trying to eat here!"

Rosa and I turned to Bubba.

"Would you please go somewhere else?!" I

said sternly.

Bubba shrugged.

"I have nowhere else to go."

"I can think of a place," I muttered.

Rosa giggled.

"Be nice," she whispered.

"He's so annoying," I whispered back. "You're leaving soon."

I looked at my watch.

"We only have two more hours, then you have to go," I reminded Rosa.

Her eyes looked sad.

"I want to spend these last two hours with you," I told her. "Alone."

We looked at Bubba.

"Well," she said. "If I go for the job, and get it, I'll have to move back here."

That made me smile.

Imagine. Rosa in Peaceville.

Life would be great.

"Then we'll have all the time we want together," she added.

## Taking Names and Kicking Assets

Bubba waved his hand between us.

"Guys, please, I'm *trying* to *eat*!" he said.

I stared at him.

"You two are weirding me out," he added.

I kept staring.

"Can't you guys talk like that when you're alone?!" he asked.

I looked from Bubba to Rosa.

Then back to Bubba.

"We're never alone!" I shouted at him.

But do you think he got the hint?

No.

Boy, he had a way of getting under my skin!

I was about to say something.

Something I would regret, I'm sure.

But I was stopped.

Because just then, there was a knock at the door.

Bubba was already here. So how much worse could this new person be?

I was hoping it was a customer.

It wasn't.

## Chapter 3

Two hours.

That was it.

That's all I had left with Rosa.

Then she had to go back to her home.

Her *other* home.

Not her dad's home in Peaceville, but instead, her home that was away from me.

All I wanted was to be with her.

*Alone.*

I did not want Bubba around.

I didn't want *anyone* around.

But if there was one person I *really* didn't want

## Taking Names and Kicking Assets

around, that person would be the person standing at my door.

The very person I did *not* want to see.

I almost didn't believe it.

The timing was *so* bad, it couldn't have gotten worse.

I wondered if I was imagining things.

I must be.

Because I don't think *anyone's* luck could be that bad.

Not even mine!

"Aren't you going to ask me in?" she said.

"I'd rather not," I said.

"Stop being silly," she said.

"I'm not being silly. You asked me a question, and I answered," I said.

Rosa called to me from the kitchen.

"Who's at the door, Dan?" she asked.

Then Rosa laughed.

"Is it Judge Simpkins?" Rosa asked. "Because if it is, you can tell him I don't know if I want to hug him or shoot him."

I heard Bubba crack up.

Then I heard Rosa laugh.

She made a light, tinkling sound.

I didn't answer, so I guess they got curious.

I say that because Rosa and Bubba came out of the kitchen.

They looked at the woman at the door.

The drop-dead gorgeous woman at my door.

Bubba threw the potato chip bag on the ground.

Then he wiped his greasy hands on his black pants.

And if the pants didn't soak up all the grease, he then wiped his hands on his black shirt.

He was leering at the woman at the door.

Then he licked his lips.

I think he was trying to get any stray chips off his lips, but it looked, well... dirty.

Not dirty as in messy.

He looked like a perv... if you know what I mean.

"Who is *that*?!" Bubba asked.

## Taking Names and Kicking Assets

I didn't know how to answer.

So I said nothing.

I was still looking at Rosa.

"Hello there, babe," Bubba said to the woman. "You looking for a date?"

The woman at the door made a noise, like she was totally disgusted.

Then she looked right at Bubba.

"Gross!" she said loudly.

Then she turned.

Her blond hair floated in an arc. It seemed to move in slow motion.

Or maybe I was imagining that.

Or losing my mind.

Or both.

All I know is that she left.

Thank goodness.

I was so relieved.

The next thing I heard was the sound of a car door slamming.

Then I heard a car peel out.

Patti would do that when she was angry.

She thought it was very dramatic.

I just thought it wrecked the tires.

I looked at Patti's car as she took off.

It was a top-of-the-line Lotus Elise. A great little car, but I wondered where she got it from. I'm sure *I* had paid for it, somehow.

It sure was a nice car, but Patti was ruining the tires by peeling out like that. And those weren't cheap tires.

But I really shouldn't care about the tires on Patti's car right now. In fact, I didn't care.

I only cared about Rosa.

I turned toward Rosa.

"So I guess that's Patti?" Rosa asked.

"Yes," I said softly.

Rosa looked small. And pale.

She also looked upset.

"Man, she's a looker, Dan," Bubba said.

I turned to Bubba.

It was hard to take my eyes away from Rosa.

I didn't want her to feel intimidated, or sad, or upset.

## Taking Names and Kicking Assets

I'm sure she was confused.

I say that because *I* was confused.

And *I* was knee-deep in this whole mess.

But Rosa was on the outside, looking in.

So she *had* to feel confused.

But I didn't want her to.

Yet, it was still too early to tell her how I felt about her.

"Yes," I said to Bubba. "I guess."

"You *guess*?!" Bubba choked out. "She's as hot as Mel. Maybe hotter! And Mel's a supermodel."

I shrugged.

"It's just outside looks," I said.

I was hoping that Rosa would get my drift.

I wanted her to know that Patti's looks didn't affect me. Well, not anymore.

They *used* to affect me.

But not anymore.

## Chapter 4

"I didn't know she was that pretty," Rosa said softly.

"Me neither, bud," Bubba said.

He wiggled his eyebrows, then he whistled.

"You *dog*," he said.

He tried to give me a high five.

I felt like decking him.

There was only one way to keep Bubba from talking.

At least only one way that *I* knew of.

And that was to put food in his big, stupid mouth.

## Taking Names and Kicking Assets

"Still hungry?" I asked him.

"Sure am," he drawled.

"How about going to Hilda's? My treat."

"Cool," Bubba said. "Are you guys coming, too?"

I took out my wallet.

I peeled off a ten dollar bill.

"No," I said. "We're good. You can go alone."

I gave him the money.

"I hope that's enough," he said. "I sure am hungry!"

I gave him a strong look.

"But don't worry," he said. "If I need more, I'll just kick it in myself."

I rolled my eyes.

"Thanks," I said. "Because I was so worried."

Rosa giggled.

I turned to her and winked.

"Okay," Bubba said. "I'll see ya, Rosa."

"Goodbye, Bubba."

I pushed him toward the door.

"Drive safe, you hear?" Bubba said to Rosa.

I slammed the door on his back before Rosa could answer.

I had one hour and forty-five minutes left with Rosa.

She *had* to leave in one hour and forty-five minutes. If she didn't, she would drive in the dark.

I didn't want her to drive in the dark.

Well, to be honest, I didn't want her to leave at all.

I was thinking those thoughts when I said, "You have to go back to work."

She nodded. "Yes."

"You are only on vacation."

"Yes," she repeated.

I walked over to her and gave her a big hug.

"It wasn't much of a vacation for you," I said.

I held her close.

My heart started thumping in my chest.

When she was near, she did that to me.

I just hoped she couldn't hear it.

## Taking Names and Kicking Assets

"Are you kidding?!" she squealed. "We saved Rico's life!"

She was beaming.

"But was that a good *vacation*?" I asked.

She smiled.

"I got to spend it with *you*, didn't I?!"

I grinned.

"And we went on a boat," she said.

"A stolen boat," I corrected.

"But it was still fun," she said.

"We chased a *killer*," I said.

She shrugged.

"He wasn't *really* a killer," she said.

I had to laugh.

"You're really a very positive person," I said.

I gave her a hug.

"I'm going to miss you," I said.

"I'm going to miss you too," she said.

She took my hand, and then guided me over to the couch.

She pointed to the couch and told me to sit down. So I sat down.

She sat next to me.

She was sitting very close to me.

I put my arm around her shoulder, and she leaned into me.

She put her head on my shoulder.

"I'm a little worried," she said.

"About what?" I asked.

"Patti."

Wow. That was getting things right out in the open.

"You don't have to worry about her, Rosa."

"But I *am* worried."

"*She's* the one who left *me*," I said.

"That's right, Dan. You didn't leave her. She left you."

"Oh wait," I said. "I think that came out wrong. I meant that she doesn't *want* me, so you don't have to worry."

"You're wrong about that, Dan. She *does* want you. That's why she's back."

I didn't believe that for a second.

"That's ridiculous, Rosa. How could you

# Taking Names and Kicking Assets

possibly even think that?" I asked.

"I can just tell," Rosa said softly.

"Woman's intuition?" I asked.

I gave her a quick kiss on the top of her head.

"That's right," she said.

She was smiling.

"Well, I hate to burst your bubble," I said.

She looked up at me.

"You probably have it all wrong, Rosa," I said. "Plus, Patti is *not at all* like you."

Rosa tilted her head.

"What does *that* mean?!"

"She's more like a pit bull."

Rosa laughed.

"And you forgot one key thing," I said.

"What's that?" she asked.

"I'm out of money, so she has no use for me."

Rosa laughed.

Then she gave me a saucy look.

"I could come up with a few uses," she said coyly.

I grinned right before our lips met.

## Chapter 5

It was time for Rosa to go, so I packed her stuff in her car.

She got into her car, then she opened her window.

"Well, I guess this is it," she said.

"I guess," I said sadly.

I handed her a bag.

"What's this?" Rosa asked.

"Some food, for later."

She opened the bag and peered inside.

Then she burst out laughing.

"You are a good man, Dan Corbett," she said.

## Taking Names and Kicking Assets

She took out one of the candy bars I had stashed in there.

She started to unwrap it as if she was going to eat it.

I grinned.

"Hey," I said. "That's for later."

She took a big bite as she grinned up at me.

"Well," she said as she finished the candy bar. "I have a saying: *better sooner than later*."

I had to smile.

"If that's when you'll come back again—sooner than later—I *like* that saying," I said.

"Keep giving me bags of candy, Dan, and I *will* be back sooner than later," she said.

"Good," I said. "Oh, wait a minute."

I turned to run back into the office.

"Don't go away," I called over my shoulder.

I heard Rosa laugh.

I ran in to my kitchen and threw open the cabinet under the sink. It was my hiding spot from Bubba. He'd never look under the kitchen sink.

I grabbed what I wanted, and ran back out to

Rosa.

"I forgot something," I said.

"What?" she asked.

I handed her another bag.

She took it and looked inside. She threw her head back and roared with laughter.

I grinned widely.

"You said that if I did that, you would come back sooner."

She patted the giant bag of candy bars I just gave her.

"I'll keep these right next to me," she said.

She put the bag on the passenger seat.

"Within arm's reach," she added.

*Hm,* I thought. *That's exactly where* **I** *wanted to be.*

I reached in her window and put my hand on hers.

"Don't give up on me, Rosa," I said softly.

"I won't," she said, just as softly.

"I just need to work this Patti thing out."

"It's okay, I understand," she whispered.

## Taking Names and Kicking Assets

But she still looked worried.

That made me feel bad because I didn't want her to be upset.

So I was surprised by what she said next.

"Keep an eye on Bubba," she said.

I frowned.

"You *know* that's a two-person job," I said.

Rosa laughed.

"Yes," she said. "That's true."

"And while they are doing it, *both* people want to kill themselves," I said.

We both laughed at that.

But then the laughter died down.

I realized what we were doing.

We were grabbing at anything in order lighten the moment.

So I figured I'd keep going with that.

After all, if I didn't laugh... I'd cry.

That's how much I was going to miss her.

"Well," I said. "Bubba *is* a pain in the butt. And he *is* an idiot. But he's ***my*** idiot. So yes, I'll keep an eye on him."

## Chapter 6

I could still hear Rosa laughing as she drove off.

I went to find Lucky.

He was out in the yard.

I think he didn't want to see Rosa driving away either, because I found him so far away.

Like I keep saying, he's a smart dog.

"Want to play ball?" I asked him.

He barked, then he ran off.

He came back about ten seconds later, with a ball.

"Good boy," I said.

## Taking Names and Kicking Assets

I had no idea where the balls disappear to.

I knew I just bought about four dozen balls for the dogs, but they were scattered all over the junkyard.

The dogs, though, knew *exactly* where all the balls were.

I tossed the ball for Lucky about fifty times.

Other dogs came over to play.

They also brought their own balls.

I guess the old Junkyard Dan had trained them to do that. I figured he felt that he was too old to go searching around for balls.

For whatever reason, I was glad the dogs had learned to do that because *I* didn't want to fetch a ball, either.

After about an hour of that, my arm was getting tired.

Plus I needed a shower.

I had a ton of dog slobber on my hands and pants. My pants looked like they had been slimed.

"Come on in, guys," I said to the dogs.

They followed me back to the office.

"I'll get you some cold water," I said.

I took the hose and filled their water dishes.

Then I sprayed a few of the dogs because some of them were really sweaty.

"Does that feel good?" I asked the dogs.

Lucky walked over to me.

"Yes," I said. "Don't worry. I'll wash you down too, Lucky."

I swear he smiled at me.

Everyone was cooled off and had some water, so it was time for me to wash up.

As I took off my dirty clothes, I turned on the TV.

I was shocked by what I saw!

A picture of Rosa was splashed across the screen.

"*Local girl solves serial murder case,*" a pretty lady said.

Then the camera went to a man with plastic hair. But Rosa's picture was still up on a corner of the TV screen.

"*Rosa Cruz, born and raised right here in*

## Taking Names and Kicking Assets

***Peaceville, is a hero...***" he said.

I picked up the phone.

I dialed Rosa's cell.

"Hello?" Rosa answered.

"Hey," I said. "You're on TV!"

Rosa laughed.

"I am?" she said.

"Yes," I said. "And now I miss you even more than I did an hour ago."

Rosa laughed.

"I thought playing with the dogs would help," I said. "So I've been playing catch with them."

"And did it help you stop missing me?" she asked.

"For a little while. But now I'm covered in dog slobber."

Rosa laughed.

"Yummmm," she said.

"So I came in to shower, and turned on the TV. And there you were."

"What are they saying?" she asked.

I turned up the volume.

"They're saying that you solved the serial murder case. And that you have thrown in your name to run for sheriff."

"Well," she said. "*I* didn't throw in my name."

"True," I said. "But I'm glad Bubba and Judge Simpkins did."

"So you really think I should run?" she asked.

Of *course* I did, but it wasn't up to me.

"It's up to you," I said.

"Do *you* want me to run?" she asked.

"Yes!" I said.

"So it's settled," she said softly.

I was smiling so hard, I thought my face would crack in two.

"So what happens now?" I asked.

"Well," she said slowly. "I guess I'll have to take a leave of absence from my job."

I held my breath.

"And you'll come back here?" I asked.

"Yes. To start the campaign," she said. "But first I'll need to find a campaign manager."

## Chapter 7

"I'll do it," I said.

"You will?" she asked. "It's a *lot* of work!"

I didn't care about that.

I just cared that I would be able to spend lots of time with Rosa.

"Do you have to spend a lot of time with the campaign manager?"

Rosa giggled.

"Day and night," she replied.

"Then I'm your man," I said.

I heard Rosa catch her breath.

I could have sworn she whispered, "Let's

hope."

But I wasn't sure.

"Hang on," Rosa said. "I have another call coming in."

I turned up the sound on the TV while I waited for Rosa.

They were talking about the murders again.

"*Word just in,*" the pretty lady on the TV said.

The lady placed her hand to her ear.

It looked like she was trying to hear something being said through an earphone.

"*Rosa Cruz needs a lot of signatures to be put on the ballot for the election in November. She's starting the race late, folks, so if you want this local hero to be your next sheriff, please let us know!*" the pretty lady said.

"*And we're told that local law enforcement is endorsing this candidate,*" the man with the plastic hair said.

The lady touched her ear again.

"*My goodness,*" she said. "*Word is just in that*

## Taking Names and Kicking Assets

*local educators are also backing this candidate!"*

The man with the plastic hair looked shocked.

*"We've just received a call from the local legal board. The legal community is behind Rosa Cruz as well,"* he said.

The man touched his ear and nodded.

*"And that's not just the lawyers!"* the man continued. *"The judicial set is also backing Rosa Cruz!"*

*"The other candidates must be sweating now, Reggie,"* the pretty lady said to the man with the plastic hair.

Rosa got back on the line.

"Dan, are you still there?" she asked.

"Yes, I'm here," I said.

"That was Judge Simpkins. He said that he has to go down and pay my qualifying fee so I can be put on the ballot."

"Wow," I said. "So it's official."

"Looks that way," Rosa said.

She giggled nervously.

"Did you mean what you said about being my

campaign manager?"

"Sure did."

"Then can you do me a favor?" she asked.

"Anything."

"Can you go with the judge and pay my fee so I can be put on the ballot?"

"Of course," I said.

"I'll pay you back," she said.

I laughed.

"I'm your campaign manager; *I'll* pay for that."

"Well," she said. "We'll discuss that some other time. All I know is that a judge can't pay it. It would look hinky. Like I'd be in the judge's pocket; if you know what I mean."

"Yes," I said. "I get it. I'll ask the judge where to go and how much money to bring."

My phone beeped.

"I think I have a call coming in," I said.

"That'll be Judge Simpkins," Rosa said. "He said he'd call you right away. I'll get off the phone so you can get that."

## Chapter 8

It wasn't Judge Simpkins.

"Dan, I'm coming right over," Patti said.

I groaned aloud.

I couldn't believe that I hung up with Rosa so Patti's call could come through.

I was not happy about that.

"Patti, I can't talk to you right now. And you can't come over. I'm waiting for a call, then I have to go out."

"From that *woman*?!" Patti spit out.

"Not that it's any of your business," I said.

"But that 'woman' has a name, and it happens to be Rosa."

"Whatever," Patti said with contempt.

"And no," I said. "Thanks to *you*, I just hung up with Rosa. But I am expecting a call from someone else, and then I'll have to leave right away."

"Aren't you the busy little beaver," she said.

She barely hid her disgust.

But I didn't think she was trying all that hard.

"Who would have known that running a junk shop made one so busy!"

Then she laughed, making her sound like the Wicked Witch of the West.

"It amazes me that *that* many people want to buy junk."

"I don't sell junk, Patti," I said through gritted teeth.

"Oh," she said. "Then I must be confused. Please enlighten me."

"I own a junkyard, Patti. An auto junkyard. I sell old cars and used car parts."

## Taking Names and Kicking Assets

"And how is that not considered junk?" she asked.

I didn't know if she was being mean or if she was just that dense.

My phone beeped.

A call was coming in.

"I have to go, I have a call coming in."

"From that, ah, *woman*?"

Patti was starting to get to me.

I was getting very annoyed.

I wanted to let Patti know that she should not mess with Rosa.

"That 'woman' is running for sheriff," I said.

I thought that would scare Patti, so I was surprised by her reply.

"Ha," she scoffed. "Kind of a *manly* woman, is she?"

I was so angry, I was afraid of what I would say.

But I wanted to take the high road, so I just hung up.

## Chapter 9

I went with Judge Simpkins to pay Rosa's qualifying fee.

I told them I was her campaign manager.

The man behind the desk looked at me.

"As her campaign manager, you should be careful."

"Why is that?" I asked.

"The man who *thought* he had the election for sheriff in the bag is *very* angry."

"And who would that be?" I asked.

"Carl Taggart."

"And why should I be careful?" I asked.

## Taking Names and Kicking Assets

The man snorted a laugh.

So did Judge Simpkins.

"Let's just say he *really* wants to win," the man said.

"I'm sure he does," I said. "So does Rosa."

"Yes, I'm sure," the man said. "But she wouldn't do *anything* to win."

The judge cleared his throat.

I looked at the judge, and he nodded ever so slightly.

That made me take notice.

"What kinds of things would this Carl Taggart fellow do?" I asked.

"He'd be the first to run a smear campaign," the man said.

I looked back at the man.

"Rosa has nothing to hide," I said easily.

"Everyone has something to hide," Judge Simpkins said. "At least everyone has things that they don't want the *world* to know."

I looked back at the judge.

"Even Rosa?" I asked.

"Sure. Rosa, you, me, even him, I'm sure," the judge said as he stabbed a finger in the air at the man behind the desk.

The man laughed heartily.

"You can say that again," the man said.

Then he looked up at me.

"Just be careful, Dan. That's all I'm saying. Rosa may be a lawyer, but she's still young. I knew her dad. He was a good man. And Rosa will be a good sheriff because she's smart, honest and kind. But Carl Taggart eats people like Rosa for breakfast, so... just be careful, okay?"

I nodded.

"Okay," I said. "I will."

"Good," the man and Judge Simpkins said at the same time.

"Do you know the process?" the man asked.

I had to laugh.

"I just got the job ten minutes ago."

"But he'll be caught up to speed by the end of the day," Judge Simpkins told the man. "Dan here is a smart one, and I'll clue him in."

## Taking Names and Kicking Assets

I smiled at the judge.

"In a nutshell, the election is in November, with the winner taking office in January."

I got excited.

"So Rosa might live here full time by January?" I asked the judge.

"If we play our cards right, she'll be here long before that, son."

"Maybe even before the election in November?"

"The sooner she plants roots in the area, the better. She'll be a local girl again," the man said.

"And that will be one less thing Carl Taggart can use against her," the judge added.

"Well, she was just telling me today that she has a saying," I said.

"What's that, son?" the judge asked.

*"Better sooner than later."*

The three men laughed.

"Well, there you go," the judge said with a smile.

## Chapter 10

I stopped at Hilda's on the way back.

Bubba and Henry were sitting at a booth.

"Hey," Bubba said. "We were just talking about you."

"Oh yeah?" I asked. "What about me?"

"Your wife is *hot*!" Bubba said.

Bubba pointed at Henry.

"I think she might even be hotter than Mel, and we all know that Mel's a super-model!"

"There's a lot more to Mel than just her looks," Henry said.

He was trying to make a point.

## Taking Names and Kicking Assets

"I didn't marry Mel just for her looks," he added.

"But they sure don't hurt!" Bubba said.

"Has anyone ever told you that you're a pig?" Henry asked Bubba.

Bubba laughed.

"Well, I'm just sayin'," Bubba said. "You both have very hot women, you lucky dogs."

"Is there a point you're trying to make, Bubba?" I asked.

Henry snorted a laugh and shook his head.

"Just that your women are good looking," Bubba said.

I tried not to look annoyed.

"Well, Bubba, I hate to burst your bubble about things, but did you hear what Henry said?"

"Not really," Bubba said with a grin.

"He said that there's a lot more to Mel than just her looks."

"So?" Bubba asked me.

"Well, I hate to admit it, and I also hate to have to be the one to tell you, but there's not much else to Patti *besides* her looks."

"I could deal with that," Bubba said.

Henry shook his head and wiped his hand over his eyes.

"It's no use," Henry said. "We're never going to change him."

That made me laugh.

"That's most likely true," Bubba said. "Which brings me to my question."

Bubba looked at me.

"Now don't get mad at me or anything, Dan," Bubba said.

Already, I didn't like the sound of this.

"But?" I asked Bubba.

"Well, you think she'll like *me*?" Bubba asked me.

Henry groaned and slapped his hand over his eyes again.

I just stared at Bubba.

"Look," Bubba said. "Just hear me out. You remember that roofer guy, right?"

I felt my eyes close to small slits.

## Taking Names and Kicking Assets

I heard Henry curse softly.

I didn't know where Bubba was going with this, but already I wasn't liking it.

"What about him?" I asked slowly.

"Well, she was slumming it when she went off with him. Right?"

I kept staring.

"So maybe she'll keep slumming it—with me."

I thought about that for a little while before I answered.

"She *may* have been 'slumming it' with Neil," I admitted.

"See?" Bubba said with hope.

"But that doesn't mean she went *that* far over the edge," I said softly.

I didn't want to hurt Bubba's feelings, but really, he was going somewhere he couldn't *possibly* know about.

Somewhere kind of dark.

But Bubba had no clue.

The idea of Bubba in a relationship with Patti

was insane.

As if he read my thoughts, Henry spoke.

"She went slumming, Bubba. Not insane."

Bubba ignored Henry.

Instead, Bubba kept talking to me.

"Come on, Dan, I've never gone out with such a hot chick," he pleaded.

"I don't think she'd be so keen on being called a hot chick," I told Bubba.

"I'd never call her that to her *face*," Bubba said boldly.

"Well that's good," I said.

"No way, man! You *never* tell a hot chick she's hot! That would just make her all full of herself!"

I thought to myself, *Patti's **always** been full of herself. Nothing anyone says or does is going to change that.*

But I didn't say that out loud.

"Plus, it would give her the upper hand," Bubba added.

Henry started cracking up.

Loudly.

# Taking Names and Kicking Assets

He shook his head.

"I've got to tell you, Bubba," Henry said. "How you end up with *any* woman is a mystery to me."

"Hey," Bubba said. "Women *beg* for me!"

"Yeah," Henry said. "They beg you to leave."

"Or they beg you to shut up," I added.

Henry and I laughed.

Bubba didn't.

Of course, that's when Patti walked into Hilda's diner.

## Chapter 11

Patti saw me, and started walking right to my table.

She pointed at me.

"You're not getting away from me *this* time!" she said angrily.

"Your goose is cooked, man!" Bubba said. "I've *got* to see this."

Bubba laughed out loud.

"She is *sexy* when she's mad," Bubba said.

I wouldn't call it sexy.

It was more like scary.

Patti was *very* scary when she was mad.

## Taking Names and Kicking Assets

Well, the correct word was angry.

Then I snorted with the thought, because when Patti was angry, she *did* get mad.

Mad as in insane.

*That's* how scary Patti got when she was angry.

But I sure wouldn't call it sexy. Not by a long shot.

Maybe Bubba thought insane was sexy.

I looked at Bubba.

Yeah, I wouldn't put it past him.

He *was* a bit insane himself.

I looked at Patti. Her face was contorted with anger.

She looked like one of those big, black storms out in the distance. The ones where you worried about your safety.

Like a tornado funnel—all dark and serious—ready to plow down whatever got in her way.

Personally, I thought that was scary. But maybe Bubba thought that was sexy.

I knew he had a screw loose—maybe a couple

of screws loose—so maybe *he* thought she looked exciting.

But if you asked me, I'd tell you that I thought she looked... well... like Patti on a rampage.

There was no other say to say it. She looked poised to give me a beat down.

Not physically, but verbally.

And I knew that I wasn't the only one who saw the business end of an assault coming toward me.

I say that because I heard Henry mutter a curse under his breath.

"You can say that again," I whispered back to Henry.

And wouldn't you know... he *did* say it again!

## Chapter 12

"Something tells me that she has a razor sharp tongue," Henry said softly.

"Oh yes," I confirmed.

That was all we could say before Patti arrived at the table.

She stood with her hands on her hips.

Gazing up at her angry face was like gazing at the sun.

It hurt if you did it too long.

Also, it could cause major damage.

I swung my eyes to Bubba.

He was staring up at Patti without caution.

He was grinning widely.

The man was a fool. He had no feel for danger.

Plus, I had the feeling he was going to make this encounter worse.

Bubba had a way of making *every* encounter worse.

"I'll give you a dollar to get lost," I said to Bubba.

Bubba grinned.

"Nah," he said.

"Five," I offered.

"Nope."

"Ten."

"No."

"Twenty?" I asked.

"No."

"Thirty."

Bubba shook his head. But his eyes never left Patti.

"Fifty," I said.

"Nope."

# Taking Names and Kicking Assets

Bubba was still grinning.

"That's my final offer," I said.

Bubba stopped grinning.

"Sold!" Bubba said loudly.

He held out his hand.

I slapped a ten and two twenties on it.

"See ya," he called out as he left.

Then I turned to Patti.

"Why are you here?" I asked her.

Patti looked at Henry.

"Do I know you?" she asked.

Of *course* she didn't know Henry. It was Patti's snobbish way of letting me know that she didn't want strangers around to hear what she had to say.

## Chapter 13

"Hi," Henry said. "I'm Henry Pake. I'm a friend of Dan's."

Henry held out his hand to Patti.

She didn't take it.

"Henry is the town librarian," I said.

Patti made a face.

"A librarian," she mumbled.

She did not look impressed.

When Patti did not shake his hand, Henry pulled his hand back.

It was all very awkward, and I was embarrassed by Patti's behavior. Embarrassed and angered by

# Taking Names and Kicking Assets

it.

"Well, I guess I should be going," Henry said.

I looked at his half-eaten plate of food.

Then I got even angrier that Patti would make him stop his meal, so she could talk to me alone.

She could plainly see that he wasn't finished with his meal.

Hilda must have noticed it too.

"Dan? Why don't you and... your guest... come sit over here," Hilda called from a booth on the other side of the room.

She was setting up the booth for two people.

I watched as Hilda put down the silverware, the coffee cups and two glasses of water.

"Please stay and finish your meal," I said to Henry.

Henry shrugged.

"Okay," he said good-naturedly.

He looked up at Patti.

"It was nice to meet you, Patti," he said.

Again, he put out his hand to shake hands.

Again, Patti did not take it.

And she didn't return his pleasantries, either.

I was getting so angry, I could feel my own blood pressure going up.

Henry took the high road.

He was pleasant and courteous and respectful.

Patti, on the other hand, was unpleasant, discourteous, and disrespectful.

She embarrassed me. And it was a shock for me to see her for who she truly was.

For the first time, I was seeing her true colors.

And it shamed me.

Shamed me for not seeing them before.

Shamed me for not realizing the kind of person she was.

And shamed me for the way she was treating my friends.

## Chapter 14

Patti turned and walked over to the booth.

As I got up from the table, I looked at Henry.

"I'm sorry for her rudeness," I said softly.

"You're not the one who was rude," he said.

Again, the man took the high road.

"And you can't control what she says or does," Henry added. "Just as no one can control what Bubba says or does."

Due to the truthfulness of that comment, Henry made me feel better.

I smiled at my friend.

"Thank you for understanding," I said.

Henry nodded.

His eyes flicked toward Patti.

"Good luck with that," he said.

I scoffed.

"Thanks. Something tells me I'm going to need it."

Henry nodded again.

I turned to join Patti at the booth.

I saw her pull the napkin off the table and then wipe down the seat of the booth.

I was worried that Hilda had seen her too.

So I looked around for Hilda.

Yes, she had seen Patti, just as I had seen her.

The look on Hilda's face was a mixture of embarrassment, confusion, insult and anger.

I *had* to protect Hilda.

"What are you *doing*?!" I said loudly to Patti.

Patti turned to face me.

"Who knows who's been sitting there?!" she said with disgust. "And who knows how clean—or dirty—this place is."

That infuriated me.

## Taking Names and Kicking Assets

"Hilda keeps a spotless place!" I roared. "And the people who come to this establishment are good, clean, honest, *respectful* people!"

As I was saying that, I arrived at the table.

I grabbed the napkin from Patti's hand. I balled it up and enclosed it with my fist.

In my lifetime, I've been angry, but I couldn't remember ever being *this* angry.

How dare she insult and degrade my friends like this!

Who did she think she was?! The Queen of England?!

I had news for her, the Queen of England would have more class and grace in her little pinky than Patti had in her entire body!

It took every cell in my body to have patience with this woman.

"Sit down," I said between gritted teeth.

Patti sat down.

I was seething with rage, but I would not let her make me say or do something that I would regret.

I had never hit a woman, and never would.

I had never hurt someone intentionally, and hoped I never would.

But it took every ounce of strength I had to control myself.

I would not lose my self control.

I would not let her bring me down to that level.

A man—a *real* man—doesn't let others have control of their anger.

And a *good* man doesn't hit a woman, no matter how much they provoke him to do so.

I dropped the balled-up napkin on the table.

"We need to talk," I said as calmly as I could.

## Chapter 15

Hilda came over and took the napkin off the table.

Hilda didn't look at Patti.

So I wondered if Hilda saw Patti take the napkin from my side of the table.

I watched, with horror, as Patti started to wipe down her fork, knife and spoon.

Hilda *must* have seen what Patti was doing, because she waited for Patti to finish, and then took the napkin when Patti had put it down.

"What are you doing?!" I said with anger. "The utensils are clean!"

"How do *you* know?" Patti asked.

"Because I come here every day," I stated.

I looked up at Hilda.

I felt terrible for the way she was being insulted.

"And because Hilda is my friend," I added. "And I know that she runs a *very* clean diner!"

"May I take your order?" Hilda asked.

She too was taking the high road.

I'll bet she wanted to take one of the glasses of ice water sitting on the table and felt like throwing it in Patti's face.

But Hilda would never do that.

She had too much class.

Too bad Patti didn't match Hilda's class.

Why hadn't I ever seen this side of Patti before?

Most likely because I had never taken her to anything but a five-star restaurant.

A four-star restaurant wasn't even good enough for Patti.

Why hadn't I seen this about her?

# Taking Names and Kicking Assets

Was I that enthralled by her looks?

Had I really been that bewitched? Captivated? Beguiled?

How could I have been that **blind**?!

They say that love can blind a person. But my God, where had I been during that entire relationship?!

Patti barely looked at Hilda.

"I'll take a grande extra hot soy with extra foam, split shot with a half squirt of sugar-free vanilla and a half squirt of sugar-free cinnamon. Oh, and can you put that in a venti cup and fill up the room with extra whipped cream with caramel and chocolate sauce drizzled on top? Thanks."

Hilda and I stared at Patti for a long time.

It took me that long to find my voice.

"She'll have a coffee," I told Hilda. "With cream and sugar, please."

Hilda nodded. "Your usual?" she asked me.

"Yes, please."

"Apple pie?" she asked.

"Sounds great. Two slices," I said.

"A la mode, as usual?" Hilda asked.

"Yes, thanks," I said.

"You want vanilla or that Ben and Jerry's you like?" Hilda asked.

I smiled up at Hilda.

She now stocked that Ben and Jerry's ice cream I liked. Mission to Marzipan.

"Surprise me," I said with a grin.

Hilda grinned back at me.

I was glad to see her smiling again.

"No ice cream for me," Patti said. "Just the pie."

Then Patti turned to me.

"Is the pie any good?" she asked me. "Or will I need the ice cream to drown out the bad pie?"

I couldn't believe she said that in front of Hilda!

How rude could this woman get?!

"The pie is the best you'll probably ever have. And it does *not* need ice cream to enhance it. I just like my pie a la mode."

"I'll be the judge of that," Patti said blandly.

## Chapter 16

Hilda shot me a look.

I think it said, "You poor man. How can you stand it." But I wasn't sure.

So I just looked at Hilda, wiggled my eyebrows and then winked at her.

She cackled before she turned her hefty body to go to the kitchen.

"Ugh," Patti groaned. "How can you stand that woman?!"

I was just thinking the same thing, but not about Hilda.

"Why are you here?" I asked Patti.

"To get you back."

So. Rosa was right.

I never would have guessed that.

"You know, Patti, you really hurt me when you left like that."

"I'm sorry."

She didn't *sound* sorry. At least not as sorry as she *should* sound.

Not as sorry as she should sound considering the pain she'd caused.

She should be very sorry.

Very, *very* sorry.

She only sounded mildly sorry. If at all.

If you'd ask me, it wasn't sorry enough.

Her amount of sorry was good for leaving the milk out. Or eating the last piece of birthday cake when it wasn't your cake. Or forgetting to turn off the car's headlights all night long.

But it sure wasn't sorry enough for leaving me. And it sure wasn't sorry enough for hurting me so badly.

"Do you forgive me?" she asked coyly.

# Taking Names and Kicking Assets

She was pouting her lips. Striking a pose.

That pose had gotten her out of a lot of arguments during our marriage.

She looked like Marilyn Monroe. You know, that old actress.

But I now saw that the problem was that she not only looked like Marilyn Monroe, she looked like an *actress*.

Like she was playing a part or a role.

I saw that clearly now.

I'd never noticed that before.

Before, it used to work on me. Quite easily.

But now? Now it seemed like an act.

It wasn't cute or charming. Or the slightest bit sincere.

It no longer worked.

"No, Patti," I said. "I don't think I've forgiven you."

She pouted prettily.

"Are you *sure*?" she asked.

She was using her "sexy" voice.

The voice that used to end all of our

arguments.

The voice that I used to love hearing.

The voice that made me hand her the credit card.

It no longer held its spell.

In fact, I now found it annoying.

It sounded false. Rehearsed. Cloying.

Now it kind of ticked me off.

## Chapter 17

"How about cutting the sex kitten act?" I asked her.

"Excuse me?"

"Can't you talk like a normal person?" I asked.

Her face hardened.

"Like *this*?" she said coldly.

"It's better than that fake voice."

"But it won't make you *feel* better," she said in her sexy voice again.

"Nothing you could *say* could make me feel better. It doesn't matter what fake voice you use."

She glared at me.

"If that's what you want."

Her voice was cold, like ice.

"This better?" she asked.

All softness was gone, and in its place was hardened steel.

"A bit."

"Can we talk?" she asked.

"Sure," I said.

"*Now* do you forgive me?"

"No."

She got up and walked out.

She tried to slam Hilda's door behind her, but it was on a spring, so the door couldn't slam.

Her dramatic exit was ruined.

But she did peel out again, from Hilda's parking lot.

Again, all I could think of were the tires on that Lotus Elise.

As they say in the theater: Scene over.

The actress has left the building.

Hilda came to my table with the coffees and

the slices of pie.

"I didn't want to disturb you," Hilda said. "So I held off until there was a lull in the, ah, conversation."

I had to smile.

"Well, this *is* a lull," I said.

Henry must have been eaves dropping, because he laughed.

"Want me to bring your stuff back over to Henry's table?" Hilda asked.

I looked at Henry.

He smiled, nodded and waved his hand toward himself.

"Sure," I said, taking my coffee with me. "Thanks, Hilda."

I settled back at Henry's table.

"Wow," Henry said. "That woman must have been very hard to live with."

"You can say that again," Hilda said right before she cackled.

"You know, I never noticed that before," I said honestly.

Hilda cackled again.

"You must have worked all day, every day not to notice *that*!" she said.

I nodded.

"I did work hard, and worked long hours. But to tell you the truth, I never saw Patti the way I'm seeing her now."

I looked up at Hilda as she put both pieces of pie before me.

"Do you think she changed that much since she left me?" I asked.

"No!" Henry and Hilda said at the same time.

"A leopard can't change its spots," Henry said.

"That woman's a real snake in the grass," Hilda said.

Henry laughed.

"Talk about someone who pretends to be your friend while secretly doing things to harm you," Henry said. "Yes, I would think that describes Patti perfectly."

Hilda patted my shoulder.

# Taking Names and Kicking Assets

"I'll go get you more ice cream for that second slice of pie," Hilda said.

"Thanks, Hilda," I said.

Hilda went toward the kitchen to get the ice cream.

"I don't think that Patti's gone for good, though," Hilda said over her shoulder.

"You don't?" I called back. "I figure she'll be long gone after *this* encounter."

Henry shook his head.

"I don't know, Dan," Henry said.

"She made no pretense that she liked Peaceville," I said. "Or anyone in it, for that matter."

Henry laughed.

"That's for sure," he said.

"So I figure she's out of here. That was it. She tried. She failed. She's moving on," I said.

That was what I *thought*.

But I was wrong.

## Chapter 18

It seemed Patti was not done yet.

She hadn't played all her cards.

I say that because she came back.

She drove her Lotus Elise into the junkyard the next morning.

I must admit, that car *did* look out of place in the junkyard.

*Patti* looked out of place in the junkyard, too.

Lucky barked at her.

Or maybe he wasn't really barking at her. Maybe he was trying to warn me.

It seemed as if Lucky had her number.

# Taking Names and Kicking Assets

He knew—by instinct—that I needed warning. He knew I needed warning when Patti was near.

Lucky was right. I *did* need warning.

I needed to prepare myself.

I needed to harden up.

I needed to brace myself so she wouldn't walk all over me.

It now occurred to me that for *years* I had let her walk all over me. It wasn't that I was a wuss. It was because I was a nice guy. And because I was hopelessly in love with her.

I could now plainly see that Patti chewed up and spit out nice guys like me. I hadn't been smart enough to see that, but Lucky was.

And now, I was smart enough to see it, too.

Of course it was *after* she chewed me up and then spit me out. But at least I finally saw it.

She entered my office without knocking.

I tried to look unaffected.

It wasn't too much of a stretch because she didn't really have the same hold on me that she used to have.

"So," I said. "You're back."

"Yes."

"Why?" I asked.

"Because I'm not done."

"With what?" I asked.

"Getting you back."

She looked so smug and confident.

I didn't like being mean, not even to her, but I had to be honest.

"You might want to change your goals," I said.

She looked around.

"I could say that to you too," she said snidely.

If she had tried to offend me, it didn't work.

"I like it here," I said.

"Why?!" she asked. She looked disgusted.

"I'm happy here."

Again, she looked around.

"You have nothing," she said.

"I have everything," I countered.

She scoffed.

"Like that idiot guy? The greasy Goth guy?"

## Taking Names and Kicking Assets

She could insult me, and I wouldn't care. But I didn't like her insulting my friends.

"Bubba's not greasy, he's a mechanic. And yes, like him."

"You paid him fifty dollars to make him leave," she reminded me.

All I could think was: *How much will it cost to get you to leave?*

Then I remembered the answer to that question.

*Everything I owned.*

# Chapter 19

I clenched my teeth. I was getting angry.

"He's my friend," I said.

She laughed at that. Or at me. I couldn't tell which.

"But you *paid* him to leave," she said.

"He's a *good* friend," I added.

Again, she laughed. "Right."

That got me going.

"Who are *you* to judge?!" I asked.

She smiled.

"Wow, Dan, this new macho-guy thing is very sexy. I like it."

## Taking Names and Kicking Assets

That was it. The last straw.

"Go," I said softly.

She sidled up beside me.

"Here?" she said. "In this dump?"

She looked around. Then she giggled.

"Does it even *have* a bedroom?" she asked.

I was in shock. How could she *possibly* misunderstand?

"Yes, this 'dump' has a bedroom. But that's not where I want you."

"Where do you *want* me?" she flirted.

I gently steered her to where I wanted her.

"Out the door," I said.

I opened the screen door with one hand, and gently guided her through the doorway with my other hand.

Then I closed the screen door.

With her on the other side.

Lucky lifted his head from where he was resting, and growled at her.

She looked shocked, but then she gathered her wits together and pulled off another movie-perfect exit.

Screeching tires and all.

When her little Lotus was gone, I looked at Lucky.

I think he smiled at me.

"That was the old ball and chain," I told him.

He just looked at me.

I think he was thinking that we all make mistakes sometimes. Either that, or he was thinking that there was no accounting for taste.

But I knew Lucky liked my latest choice.

He crawled onto Rosa's lap at every chance.

Thoughts of Rosa made me miss her.

So I went inside to call her.

She answered on the second ring.

"How are you holding up?" she asked me.

"I'm great. Why do you ask?"

"Mel told me about Patti in the diner," Rosa said.

Ah. How could I forget? Small town living. Henry is married to Mel who is best friends with Rosa.

## Taking Names and Kicking Assets

"You were right," I told Rosa. "She wants to come back. Or should I say, she wants *me* back. She wants nothing to do with Peaceville."

"Oh," Rosa said softly. "Am I going to lose my campaign manager?"

"You might *fire* your campaign manager," I said. "But he will never walk away willingly."

"Are you sure?" Rosa asked.

"I promise."

"Good," Rosa said with a hearty laugh. "Because it looks like we're on our way. We have just about all the signatures we need for me to be put on the ballot! The entire police force has been getting signatures all day. It looks like this plan is starting to shape up."

I couldn't have been happier.

"So when are you coming home?" I asked.

"I just spoke with the senior partner at the firm and handed in my notice," she said.

My heart started beating wildly.

"So when are you coming home?" I asked again. "In two weeks?"

"The senior partner said that I don't have to wait two weeks. Since I tied up all my cases before I left for vacation, there is nothing for me to do here. So I am free to leave now."

"Are you kidding?" I asked.

"Nope," she said lightly. "Tonight I will go back to my place and will start to pack up."

I held my breath as I asked my next question.

"Need an extra set of hands?" I asked.

"I'd love your help!" she replied.

"Want me to bring a moving truck?" I asked.

Rosa giggled, a light tinkling sound.

"If you have one handy," she said.

My heart thumped harder and faster than before.

This was it! She was coming home! And *I* was going to be the one to bring her home.

My heart felt buoyant.

I tried to hide my excitement, but I think I failed.

"I'm leaving right now," I said as I hung up the phone.

## Taking Names and Kicking Assets

So Rosa's coming back to Peaceville.

She will try to be elected as the local sheriff.
And Dan will be her campaign manager.

But there's one little problem...

Is Patti gone for good?
Probably not!
She doesn't seem to be the type
who gives up *that* easily.

Read the *next* book of the **Junkyard Dan** series,
***Mercy***,
to find out if
Patti is gone for good,
if Rosa wins or loses the election,
if Dan makes it through the whole mess
and if Bubba lives to tell the tale.

If you are enjoying the

# Junkyard Dan

series,
we have a few **other** series
that you might *also* like to
read...

# Want comedies?

## Try reading...

# THE
# SMITH
# BROTHERS

Come meet Les, Ling, Luiz and Bob.
They **are** "The Smith Brothers."

(And they're *completely* insane!)

# NOX PRESS
**books for that extra kick to give you more power**
**www.NoxPress.com**

Everyone has it
within them
to be a

Do **you**?

# NOX PRESS
**books for that extra kick to give you more power**
**www.NoxPress.com**

The

# LEADER

series.

# HONOR
# COURAGE
# RESPECT
# SERVICE
# INTEGRITY
# COMMITMENT
# LOYALTY
# DUTY

(We bet you can't read just one!)

# HUNGER FOR ACTION?

## Welcome to

Pete drives a lunch truck.

He's a nice enough guy,
but there's something about him
that makes his customers wonder.

And what's with the bullet holes
all over the truck?!

# NOX PRESS

**books for that extra kick to give you more power**
**www.NoxPress.com**

We also have
a funny series called:

# A LEEG OF HIS OWN

Andrew Leeg is one of a triplet. And the only boy.
So, as you've probably guessed,
the other two are girls.
Yeah, that's right. Two sisters.
Abbie Leeg and Annie Leeg.
They always bug Andrew.
And nag him like you would *not* believe!
It's always two against one. And usually, the girls win.
But Andrew always goes down fighting!
He's *truly* in...

## A LEEG OF HIS OWN

## NOX PRESS
**books for that extra kick to give you more power**
**www.NoxPress.com**

# Want to read more
# NOX PRESS
# books?

Go online to
**www.NoxPress.com**
to see what's being released!

Books can easily be purchased online
or you can contact **Nox Press**
via the Website for quantity discounts.

**Are you a fan?**

Do you want us to put *your* comments
up on our Website?
If so, please e-mail them to:
**NoxPress@gmail.com**

# NOX PRESS
**books for that extra kick to give you more power**
**www.NoxPress.com**